My Imaginative Mind

A thought-provoking Photopoetry book about aspects of the author's life dramatised through poetry, photographs, artwork, colour and reflections. Unique, yet creative storytelling with an inspirational and positive outlook on life. Experiences interwoven from the author's 4 'Pillars' of the world…. United Kingdom, South Africa, Canada, and Australia. Fun, relaxing and easy to read. A book thàt allows the reader to see a different interpretation every time.

Nadine Mackie

Self Published through Amazon KDP

My Imaginative Mind

Nadine Mackie

ISBN: 9798507416028

Copyright © 2021 Nadine Mackie.

All Photography and Artwork by Nadine Mackie.

All rights reserved. No part of this book may be copied, reprinted, shared or reproduced by any mechanical, electronic or graphic format without written permission from the author except in the case of brief quotations within fair usage.

All contents including photographs, poetry and reflections in this book are the expressed opinion of the author. The information provided in all formats is for entertainment purposes only. In the event, you use any of the information in this book for yourself, which is your constitutional right, the author and publisher assume no responsibility for your actions.

Contents

Preface

During the COVID-19 pandemic, I had time to revaluate my life. My vision of publishing a book; a challenge I could only do by stepping away from the business world. It was a difficult decision, yet I am so happy I have taken this opportunity to share aspects of my life through poetry, photographs and reflections. My mind is so full of ideas and thoughts, and I truly value the support of my friends, who at times were tough critics of my work.

Perseverance prevailed as I listened and worked hard to create visual inspiration and motivational storytelling.

I dared to be different and non-judgmental, to express my positive outlook on life. I have designed this book to illustrate my creative writing, my paintings, colouring in activities and photographs. A dream where you find your own purpose and enjoyment in life.

I invite you to sit down, relax and enjoy reading my coffee table book.

Introduction

I have always felt inspired to tell my story, to lift the energy of the world, in a way we can all understand. The vibration of looking at a photograph sets the intentions of an imaginative mind. Reading the description in verse can change your intentions, hopefully to feel a more positive vibration of good, felt energy.

I have taken my inspiration from what I call my '4 Pillars' of the world… from the United Kingdom, South Africa, Canada and Australia. The love and support of my family and friends have encouraged me to publish this book.

How to use

This book uses pictures and words to describe the world from a different angle.

Colour also plays an important role in the way you think, react and see the world. The vibrations of colours in colour therapy are said to enhance your mood and overall health.

Use the image to visualise the story and create your own meaning of the picture.

Certain sections are thoughts captured through poetry, which also have reference to scripture for a spiritually uplifting quality to encourage those looking for a deeper meaning.

Some images might encourage you to meditate; while taking a deep breath in and slowly breathing out, letting the energy flow through your body.

I have used this photograph of an apple on the beach to help change how we look at life.

An apple tossed away and lost at sea,
washed ashore and rolling in the waves.
At first sight a lovely green apple,
reflecting a shadow in the sand.
As the wave rolled the apple over,
a bad and rotten apple appeared.
Imperfection is still food for thought.
The cycle of life and death.
Treat each with respect.

Everyone has the potential for realisations in life and the opportunity to see the world in a different light. You choose how you react when life is not so perfect.

What is the first thought that enters your mind when you look at a photograph?

Write down your thoughts and feelings.

Your thoughts and visions can bring back memories and fears, be they good or bad.

You choose how you see the image or how you react to what you are feeling.

Now look at the photograph again and find a happy thought; imagine the strawberry floating up to the surface when the glass is filled with liquid, the bubbles creating movement and a journey.

Now slowly take a deep breath in.

Breathe out slowly and try to release any fears or negative thoughts you might have had when you first looked at the photograph.

Replace them with happy thoughts.

Through the eye of the lens
a whole new world is captured.
Transforming its image
to brighten up your day,
inspiring positive energy.

The photographs and poetry are there to inspire and motivate you.

Some find it relaxing and healing; others find joy and pleasure.

Looking into the glass of fizz,
watching the strawberry floating to the top.

Start the Journey

Poetry

Words of Expression are the reason I write poetry; to communicate an idea, an ideal, or a feeling. I took the photographs on this page to illustrate how words can be inspiring, different and creative.

An inscription at Dr. Sun Yat-Sen Classical Chinese Garden, Vancouver, Canada.
The Scholars Room, a project of the Rotary Club of Chinatown, dedicated to Rotary's 100 years of service.

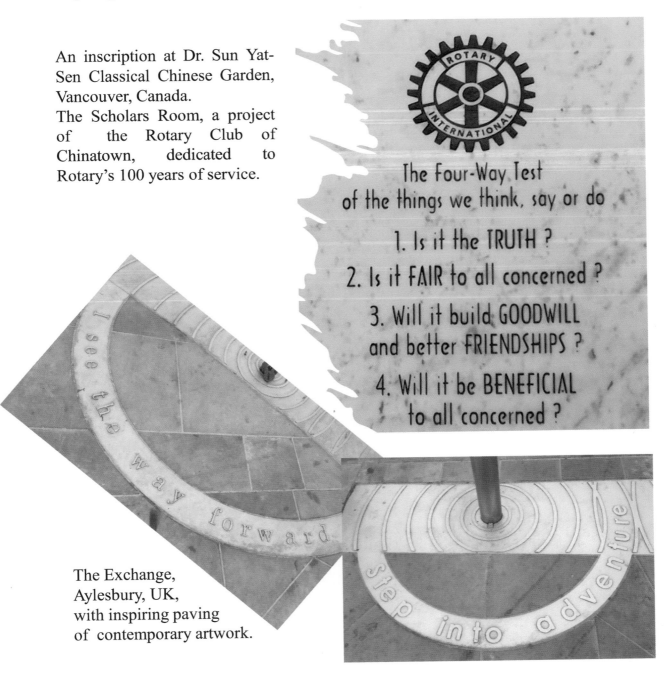

The Exchange,
Aylesbury, UK,
with inspiring paving
of contemporary artwork.

Dreaming

Beneath the light I sit,
My eyes closing,
My mind wandering,
Dreaming of our togetherness.

Sharing

My place is your place,
This hour is your hour,
My thoughts are for you,
And my life I share with you.

"To God be the glory, great things
He has done."

Hymn by Author: Frances Jane Crosby

A hymn that came to mind at the time of writing the poem 'A Vision'.

The poem was written for the Christian Centre where I used to work, entailing a journey to see the growing and vibrant 'Upper Room'. This 'Upper Room' was the coffee shop located in the Christian Centre above the Post Office, which offered a meeting place for people to enjoy a meal or a cup of coffee.

The 'Upper Room' is also mentioned in the Bible as a room above the main house for leisure and the setting of the Last Supper.

A Vision

The walls speak to you,
Lined with verse and song,
A vision of God's creation,
For today if one word brings comfort,
Tomorrow might bring joy,
And the next a spiritual cleansing,
For season upon season the void will
be filled,
Each step to 'The Upper Room'
a journey,
Vibrant and colourful the inner
beauty glows,
The mind is fed and the soul will grow,
God's light shining through
the darkness,
Unfolding into untold beauty.

Poetry Story

Jacaranda Blossoms

This poetry story is based on my experiences and a Jacaranda seed. The photographs on this page are of the Jacaranda tree in the story, grown from seed and now standing in the grounds of Weltrevreden Methodist Church in South Africa, since 2001.

The bottom left photograph shows the initial growth of the Jacaranda tree. Over the years it became hidden by shrubbery and eventually cut down. This sad feeling left me never believing growth was possible. However, the bottom right photograph shows regrowth, a tall slender tree starting to grow again.

What a miracle!

This is one scripture reflection that comes to mind:

Matthew 13: 31-32 (*Good News Bible: Today's English Version (1976). Published in South Africa by the Bible Society.*) states that

The Parable of the Mustard Seed

"Jesus told them another parable: "The Kingdom of heaven is like this. A man takes a mustard seed and sows it in his field. It is the smallest of all seeds, but when it grows up, it is the biggest of all plants. It becomes a tree, so that birds come and make their nests in its branches."

God has a plan for my life, and that's all you need to know.

Jacaranda Blossoms

On a hot summer's afternoon.
As the cool breeze filtered through
the huge Jacaranda trees,
fern-like leaves rustled
sending showers of blossoms,
like a colourful array of
violet, blue and purple confetti,
to line the streets and pavements.
A romantic setting!
'Tis the season for wedding bells.
But alas! No bride and groom today.

A Tale

Many people graced the streets
on this sweltering summer's day,
seeking the cool shade
beneath the Jacaranda trees.
Expressionless faces wandering around
chasing a dream.
Secretly, each one hoping to catch
a blossom or two.
As the tale goes, catch a blossom
and make a wish,
for it might just come true.
It's an adventure for young,
spirit filled people.

Dreams

Two friends walked beneath the trees chatting,
looking rather like a hope and have faith story.
Suddenly, the conversation came to a halt.
A blossom gently falling over my shoulder,
a blossom caught softly in my hand.
The joys of young people's dreams.
Yes, today was the day my dreams
might just come true.
A blossom I did catch and a wish I did make.
It felt like paradise.

Wedding Bells

'Tis the season for wedding bells.
That little church amongst the Jacaranda trees,
with its fern-like leaves forming a ceiling.
Handsome grey barked trunks as tall pillars,
branches forming a decorative pattern of strength.
A new beginning of love and romance.
A dream set in a scene of flowers,
wedding bliss for sure!

Adverts

It's time for those dreamy shampoo adverts.
Yes, that's me running amongst the blossoms,
on a carpet full of cool, bell-like flowers,
tossing the Jacaranda blossoms high into the air.
Then, "Cut!" A rumbling from above.
The heavens opened and blessed the land.
It's the late summer afternoon showers.
A beautiful mass of colour converged together,
flowing like a meandering stream down the streets.

A Season for All

Season to season life would bring new adventures.
It's time for seeds to glide with the wind,
anchor and nestle amongst earthy shades of autumn.
Finding nourishment and protection
during those chilly winter months.
Spring would bring life again,
as the little seed grows
reaching far beyond our wildest dreams.
A tree blowing in the breeze,
watching, yet another tale,
bringing joy to the moments of summer.
Life's little treasures.
A season for all.

A Little Seed

A little seedpod I did find and into a small pot it did go.
For many weeks I watered it patiently,
waiting for the first signs of life.
Spring would bring a little shoot, so I could watch it grow.
With care and love, it grew and grew.
A blessing for a tree with many blossoms.
This was simply no New Year's resolution,
a custom many adhered to.
Many are broken or merely forgotten about,
but this was a commitment to love and to cherish
my little Jacaranda tree, my treasure of yesterday's tale.
Walking beneath the trees, the spirit of the wind
filling the air with the joy of a tale still deep in my heart.
A blossom I did catch for a wish I do hold.

Maturity

My little seed now a little tree and too big for its little pot.
Transplanting to a bigger pot, its home for many years.
For now, I too had grown; a bridegroom I had found.
A wish made upon a falling blossom; a tale soon forgotten.
Yet, this little tree travelled to many places,
I would call home.
The signs of true maturity appeared some 15 years later.
Blossoms graced the branches of my little Jacaranda tree,
and the excitement of the tale started all over again.

Freedom

Now the world took on another look.

Thoughts of freedom came to mind,

as my pot bound Jacaranda tree

needed to spread its roots.

The day soon came with a move to another country.

Yes, it was time to move on,

but this time without my little Jacaranda tree.

Choosing a haven for my Jacaranda tree,

a sanctuary in the grounds of the Methodist church,

a home with God's people.

Yes, it was home, a place I would always visit.

It, too, had loads of memories to fill my treasure chest.

On returning home more than a year later,

I visited a tall but bushy Jacaranda tree.

Freedom had made the Jacaranda tree lose its shape.

Alas! All it needed was to be moulded and cared for.

The gentle hands of a gardener,

guiding my little Jacaranda tree.

A Wish

A wish now treasured for the tale lives on.
A tree blowing in the breeze,
watching people walking beneath its branches,
looking for yet another tale
to fill life's joyous moments.
A blossom to catch and a wish to hold.
A simple, fairy-like tale, is it?
Or just a season for all.

Life

Life's little experiences,
inspires one through a blossom.
Restores one's hope and faith,
because of a wish.
Gives life when a seed is planted.
Teaches love and care to the growing.
After a full cycle,
and many years of patience,
one is blessed with the fruit.

A Wiseman

A Wiseman tells of a new life,
the world's greatest treasure as your inheritance.
Let God plant the seed, and care for you.
He watches you grow, while you serve His kingdom,
giving you hope and faith.
God has a plan for your life and mine,
and that's all you need to know.
Yes, the church is God's bride, God is the bridegroom.
Giving to those who choose it,
a perfect inheritance is Heaven.
A simple act of nature's Jacaranda blossoms and a tale.
The truth one searches for in life, in God's time not mine.

A BLOSSOM: What an Inspiration!

A WISH: Hope and Faith

A SEED: A New Life

GROWTH: To Care and To Love

FRUIT: A Blossom

PATIENCE: It takes Many Years

Scriptural Reflections for Poems

Jacaranda Blossoms	Isaiah 35: 1 'Joy of the Redeemer' and Revelation 22: 17 'The Coming of Jesus'
A Tale	1 Timothy 4: 7-8
Dreams	1 Peter 1: 24-25
Wedding Bells	Isaiah 65: 17 and 22 'New Creations' and Isaiah 62: 5
Adverts	Leviticus 26:4
A Season for All	Matthew 13: 31-32 'The Parable of the Mustard Seed'
A little Seed	Mark 4: 26-29 'The Parable of the Growing Seed'
Maturity	Revelation 19: 7 'The Wedding Feast of the Lamb'
Freedom	2 Corinthians 3: 17
A Wish	John 8: 31-32
Life	Galatians 5: 22-23
A Wiseman	Revelation 21: 2 'The New Heaven and the New Earth' and Jeremiah 29: 11

This poetry story with scriptural reflections was adapted from my short story, 'A Jacaranda Blossom' that was published in the book called 'Memoirs of the Imaginative Mind'. This gave me the opportunity of publishing my own poetry address book with 12 poems, a wonderful gift for my family and friends.

The scriptural reflections referred to are my own personal preferences each relating to the poem, giving a deeper, spiritual meaning and insight to my poetry. Life is a journey, not a destination, so plant a seed.

Visual Story
Telling

Photography

Photography tells its own story, from colour to movement and emotions.

Visual storytelling puts you at the centre without me even expressing a single word.

Your imagination tells the story. Find peace in all aspects and enjoy the visual journey.

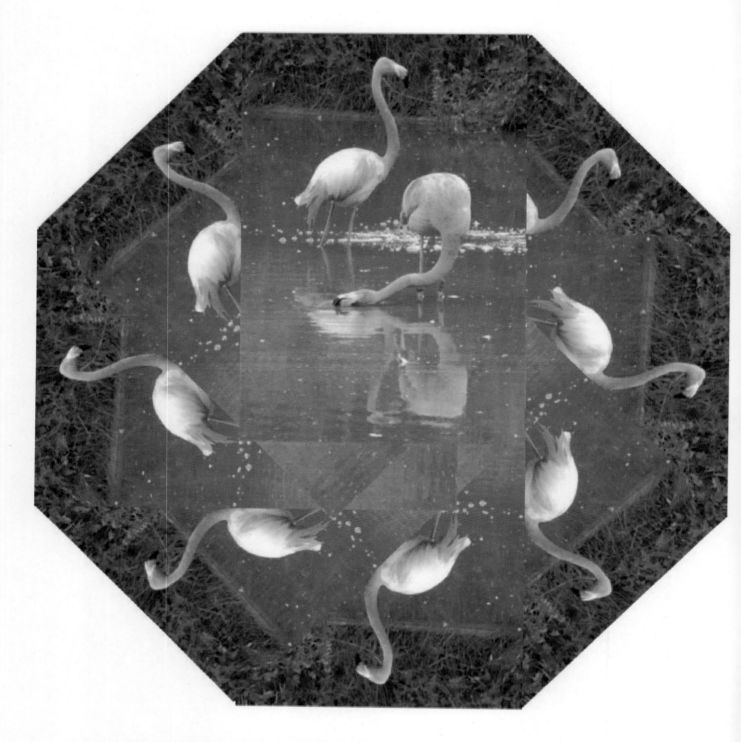

Flip and rotate photographs creating your own pattern.

Life is like a kaleidoscope of fascinating colourful patterns. Shake it up and the pattern is broken, yet when you hold it to the light, a completely different pattern emerges, just as beautiful.

My purpose as a photographer is to use my creative ability to communicate through my photographs, showing expression and meaning.

Colours inspire me as they create such an energy from feelings of happiness to sadness.

Unusual subjects are intriguing and can make conversations interesting.

This photograph was much debated about. Is it trick photography? No, just luck. The light and reflection in the water droplet created an image that looks like an alien or a sailor with his cap on. Unexplained!

UK
Landscapes

Sissinghurst Castle Garden,
Kent

Lacock Abbey, Wiltshire

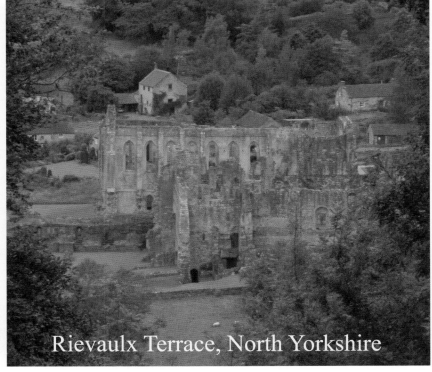

Rievaulx Terrace, North Yorkshire

Southend on Sea Pier Railway Train, East Coast

Isle of Man

Celtic Manor Golf Course, Wales

Porthkerry Beach, Wales

Cowes, Isle of Wight

The Solent channel, views of Portsmouth from Ryde

Wind farm off the coast in Great Yarmouth

Firth of Forth, Scotland is the estuary that flows into North Sea

Oil Rig in the Firth of Forth, Scotland

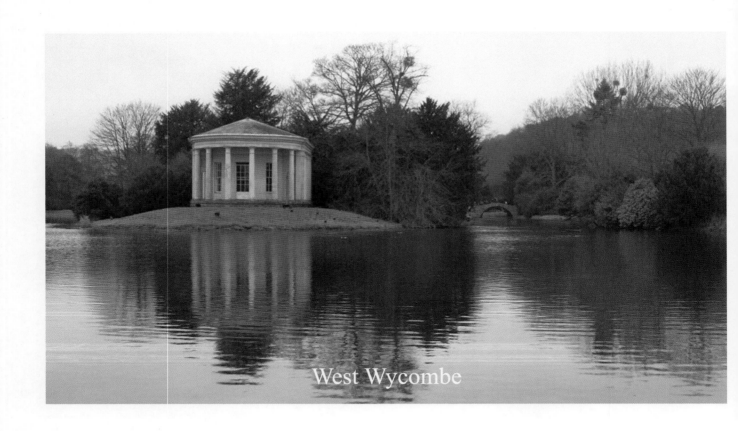

West Wycombe

Hemel Hempstead

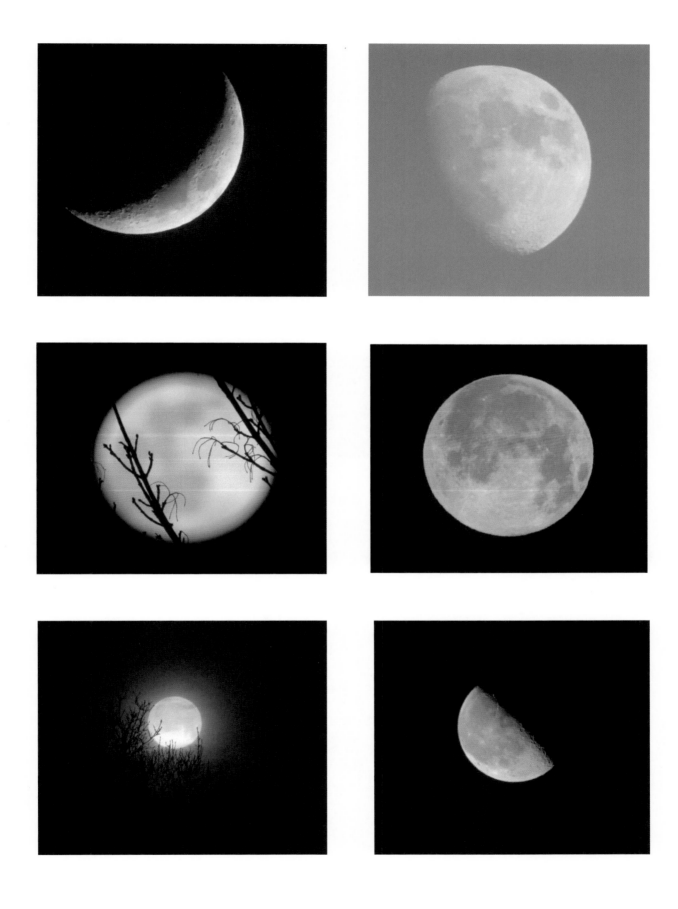

Autumn

Winter

Spring

Summer

Secret Garden

The Gate of Opportunity

Hidden Garden

57

Let Us Cross

the

Bridge Together

Photopoetry

Visual art and poetry. Combining photographs and poems triggers the imagination and expands its meaning.

A photograph has an immediate visual impact with thought provoking words.

Photography inspires expression in a poetic or vivid description.

Photopoetry intensifies a thought. Lodged in the mind, memory or emotion. Aspiring reflections long after the moment of seeing and reading.

Water Lily

New Beginnings are life's cycles.
Painted, especially for you.
The wonder of new growth,
found reflected in a Water Lily,
a flower of sheer beauty,
a bud full of wonders,
emerging out of the water.
Water the life and soul of the world.
The centre of the bloom,
is like the rays of the sun.
A source of power and energy,
reflecting its awesome beauty.
A revival and a blessing,
for the world today.

Alone

Alone in the garden of love and memories,
A place to rest your soul,
A time to acknowledge your life.
A life of passion that became your strength,
A lesson where patience tamed your passion,
Alas, your life is now a spirit,
sitting upon the seat.
A place left for others to connect
with their inner self.
A bench to sit in silence,
and feel the energy of your life.

Bobs

Hi! My name is Bobs,
A cute-looking hunk of a cat,
The male cat version, I must add,
But, what you would call a real pavement special,
Since the same stereotypes are seen around town.
I am a cat with a very good attitude,
And loads of charm, of course,
Cuddles I enjoy with my human family,
Especially, early morning when they are asleep,
I pounce onto a sleeping body and snuggle up real close,
Position my claws and knead bread till I strike flesh,
Oh dear! That hurt.

Quick, time to embrace,
Little paws around my mother's neck,
My little head tucked firmly under her chin,
She hears my gentle purring and off to sleep she goes.
That's me; a real lover not a fighter.
Fashion, well, only black tie for me,
With a fancy white bow tie and long whiskers,
Rather odd black and white socks and shoes,
But, that's style!
Strutting a rather shorter tail,
What I call a misjudgement of my speed,
You know those remote control garage doors…?
These days they are so silent and do move with speed,
A slight accident and off came a wee bit of tail.
At least I am still far from looking like a Manx.
Yes, that's me, Bobs the cat.

Reflections

Serious thought and consideration have been given to each poem or prose to reflect an inspirational message as seen in each photograph.

A personal insight is portrayed which lends to an uplifting style of contemporary poetry.

What is life without a story!

Thought I would tell you my story by giving you a little background behind my journey!

After my 2006 calendar project which I designed and had published to raise money for a charity, the decision was made to change the design and print my calendars at home. I designed and printed a single A4 sized calendar with six months on each side. Each month displayed photographs I had taken in the year before.

I enjoyed this journey and the pleasure I saw on everyone's faces when they received my calendar as a gift each year.

In 2013, my personal life changed drastically for me, and I stopped this creative journey. Everyone missed my calendar gifts. Five years later after a soul seeking journey and keen to be creative again, I started designing and printing my calendar for 2018. Year after year I felt that my creativity needed to be more expressive.

Melbourne, Australia

In 2018 I had the opportunity and travelled to countries like Australia and Canada, which I had never visited before. This opened my mind to new creativity within.

My 2019 calendar illustrated a more diverse look, highlighting my travels. A year that reflected my zest for life, celebrations, reunions, loss and sadness. I felt the time had come for me to take that leap of faith, huge step forward in my creativity. I decided to venture out of my comfort zone by designing calendars that used words to express my photographs rather than places.

Just
Love It!

My Passion is My Strength.

A dream, I have waited for,

Biding time and preparing,

Patience is Passion Tamed.

A storyboard portrayed in a book,

through visual photography,

and descriptive poetry.

Life is ... A story told,

For together we stand.

Heal our Nations.

'My Passion is my Strength'

2018 Calendars

'Patience is Passion Tamed'

2019 Calendars

My Passion
is
My Strength

There are many quotes about passion and finding your passion in life. One popular quote is "My greatest strength is my passion and my drive," as quoted by James Franklin.

'My Passion is my Strength'

I choose to put my passion,
before my strength.
Without passion it is harder,
to find the strength.
Without a purpose,
you need strength.
My passion for photography,
gave me the strength to inspire.
My strength gave me,
the determination to motivate.
My purpose,
seeing the world in a different light.

Patience is Passion Tamed

Quotation by **<u>Lyman Abbott</u>** "Patience is passion tamed."

'Patience is Passion Tamed'

A classic example,
a dream to paint,
memories from my photographs,
I bided time and prepared.
Patience got the better of me,
my passion tamed.
Years later this lesson,
inspired me to create,
a mixed media artwork.
An achievement of completion,
talent in a different art form.
Drawings, paintings, photography.
Achievements on the wall,
with space for more.

Life is ...

Like a colouring in book.
You choose your colour.
You paint your path.
You highlight a mood.
All within the lines.
The bolder the lines,
The more life stands out.
Outside the lines,
the world is,
how you see it.

A storyboard,
You see it,
You read it,
You reflect on it.

Street art in Melbourne, Australia

Choices

To make a New Year's resolution or not!
One time of the year I feel
it does not matter,
what choice I make.
It is the freedom of choice,
that is so liberating.

I choose this photograph of
an artist's expression,
a roller coaster of colourful plastic lids,
much like life full of colour,
twists and turns.
Waste not.

Love and Commitment

Such powerful words yet without,
life can feel empty.
Love is passionate and romantic.
Friendships, caring and supportive.
With love comes commitment,
a promise and dedication.
A little tender loving care,
showed through verbal expression,
serves a positive sense of purpose.
"Love conquers all"

Surprises and Strength

That look of surprise on the tiger's face,
I just cannot believe my luck,
nor could the tiger!
Patiently waiting and watching
for that unexpected
element of surprise to unfold.
The surprise could be good,
or lost, in shock or disbelief.
Through it all, the display of
profound physical strength.
Will emotional strength,
stand the test of time?

Sacrifice and Metamorphosis

At sometime during any life
sacrifices are made,
Some in vain, others for love.
Surrendering in a positive light,
a chance for a process
of transformation.

The powerful symbolic meaning
of the cross.
The metamorphosis of a butterfly.
A short life with purpose,
to bring beauty and joy to life.

Solitude and Healing

At the centre of a labyrinth,
a bench of solitude, all alone!
Yet, surrounded by healing.
Rose quartz stones,
cleansed when it rains,
energy re-charged at full moon,
the warmth absorbed from the sun,
to bring healing for those,
who rest their feet upon them stones.
Walk the path of the labyrinth,
Re-charge your energy,
Seek to gain strength
to find healing within.
An experience I cherish.

Fragile and Precious

Fragile yet robust,
Tiny yet precious.
The delicate, translucent,
fluttering wings of a dragonfly
is fast in flight.
Multi-directional viewing,
superpower, advanced vision.
An extremely efficient,
and precious insect
in indicating the quality,
of the environment.
value nature's ecosystems.
Fragile and Precious.

Adventure

Exciting and at times dangerous.
Where there is life, there is adventure.
Nothing like gliding among the clouds,
with breathtaking views,
that thrill when coming into land,
precision and timing,
the heart rate pounding,
Wishing for a safe landing.
A lesson well learnt,
an experience enjoyed.
Life is an adventure.

Guidance and Balance

The lighthouse, a beacon of light
guiding the ships at sea.
Illuminating waterways to help resolve
difficulties coming ashore.
Guidance throughout life is all part of
growing up and learning.
A balancing act of problem solving
and awareness.
The balancing of stones is
increasingly becoming popular
as a form of art or discipline.
We all can shine and bring light
and balance into the world.

Family and Community

'Birds of a feather flock together'
Just like we gather
as a family, or a community
to share moments in time.
Celebrate, comfort, care
and support each other,
for together we stand strong.
Just like this flock of flamingos,
Wading through the water,
and standing on one leg.
Charmingly compassionate.
A beautiful vision of pink.

Serenity

As I walk along the pathway,
the trees reflecting in the water,
I feel at peace, calm and untroubled.
A brief encounter with nature,
enough to bring serenity into my life.
Ready to start another day.

Mischievous

Fun loving, impish elephant,
with a mischievous smile.
I laugh at the antics,
amusing butt rubbing
and trunk scratching,
the elephant is laughing too.
Still a calf and oh! So hairy,
All good mischievous fun.

Journey and Heritage

It is the journey not the destination,
I look back on my heritage
and find we tend not to forget,
the culture through the ages.
The journey once made by ox wagon,
the tale passed down to the community,
now all that remains is the legacy.
In the grounds of a café,
a place where I would enjoy a cup of tea.

2020
Life is ...
  # 2020
Life is ...

Choices | Love and Commitment | Surprises and Strength | Adventure | Guidance and Balance | Family and Community

January

SUN	MON	TUE	WED	THU	FRI	SAT
NEW YEAR		1	2	3	4	
5	6	7	8	9	10	11
12	13	14	15	16	17	18
19	20	21	22	23	24	25
26	27	28	29	30	31	

February

SUN	MON	TUE	WED	THU	FRI	SAT
						1
2	3	4	5	6	7	8
9	10	11	12	13	14	15
16	17	18	19	20	21	22
23	24	25	26	27	28	29

March

SUN	MON	TUE	WED	THU	FRI	SAT
1	2	3	4	5	6	7
8	9	10	11	12	13	14
15	16	17	18	19	20	21
22	23	24	25	26	27	28
29	30	31				

July

SUN	MON	TUE	WED	THU	FRI	SAT
			1	2	3	4
5	6	7	8	9	10	11
12	13	14	15	16	17	18
19	20	21	22	23	24	25
26	27	28	29	30	31	

August

SUN	MON	TUE	WED	THU	FRI	SAT
						1
2	3	4	5	6	7	8
9	10	11	12	13	14	15
16	17	18	19	20	21	22
23	24	25	26	27	28	29
30	31					

September

SUN	MON	TUE	WED	THU	FRI	SAT
		1	2	3	4	5
6	7	8	9	10	11	12
13	14	15	16	17	18	19
20	21	22	23	24	25	26
27	28	29	30			

Sacrifice and Metamorphosis | Solitude and Healing | Fragile and Precious | Serenity | Mischievous | Journey and Heritage

April

SUN	MON	TUE	WED	THU	FRI	SAT
EASTER		1	2	3	4	
5	6	7	8	9	10	11
12	13	14	15	16	17	18
19	20	21	22	23	24	25
26	27	28	29	30		

May

SUN	MON	TUE	WED	THU	FRI	SAT
					1	2
3	4	5	6	7	8	9
10	11	12	13	14	15	16
17	18	19	20	21	22	23
24	25	26	27	28	29	30
31						

June

SUN	MON	TUE	WED	THU	FRI	SAT
	1	2	3	4	5	6
7	8	9	10	11	12	13
14	15	16	17	18	19	20
21	22	23	24	25	26	27
28	29	30				

October

SUN	MON	TUE	WED	THU	FRI	SAT
				1	2	3
4	5	6	7	8	9	10
11	12	13	14	15	16	17
18	19	20	21	22	23	24
25	26	27	28	29	30	31

November

SUN	MON	TUE	WED	THU	FRI	SAT
1	2	3	4	5	6	7
8	9	10	11	12	13	14
15	16	17	18	19	20	21
22	23	24	25	26	27	28
29	30					

December

SUN	MON	TUE	WED	THU	FRI	SAT
		1	2	3	4	5
6	7	8	9	10	11	12
13	14	15	16	17	18	19
20	21	22	23	24	25	26
27	28	29	30	31		
CHRISTMAS	&	BOXING DAY				

  POPPIE
Photography by Nadine Mackie ©

  POPPIE
Photography by Nadine Mackie ©

Calendar photographs:

January	Artwork at Timberlake Village, Garden Route, South Africa
February	Marabou Storks at Tenikwa Wildlife Awareness Centre, South Africa
March	Tiger at Whipsnade Zoo, UK
April	Wooden Cross at the Holy Trinity Church Belvidere, Knysna, South Africa. Butterfly from one of the Butterfly Sanctuaries
May	Bench surrounded by rose quartz stones in the centre of the Labyrinth at Ibis River Retreat, South Africa
June	Dragonfly in the Karoo, South Africa
July	Paragliding in Sedgefield, South Africa
August	Lighthouse in Barry and balancing stones in St Davids, Wales
September	Flamingos at Whipsnade Zoo, UK
October	Anglesey Abbey, Cambridge, UK
November	Elephant at Whipsnade Zoo, UK
December	Nieu Bethesda, South Africa

Calendar photographs taken in St Francis Bay, South Africa except for October.

January	Footprints on the beach
February	Geranium leaf
March	Coastal daisies on the sand dunes
April	Rainbow in the village and a mosaiced cross
May	Aloe plants growing along the coastline
June	Bottlebrush tree
July	Vygies (little figs) – Carpobrotus quadrifidus
August	Nasturtium flower
September	Geranium (Pelargonium) flower
October	Near Joubertina, South Africa
November	Daisy – Felicia amoena
December	St Francis Bay beach at low tide

On the next page the photograph on the top left is of the Illumination Trail at Blenheim Palace, Woodstock, UK. Bottom left photograph of the Praying Hands is in St Davids Cathedral, Wales, UK. The photograph on the right are peonies flowers.

Heal our Nations

Together we stand,
a pandemic year past,
And, by no means over.
Together we stand,
in memory of those
who have flown,
compassion for those
struggling,
Praying for healing,
and giving thanks.

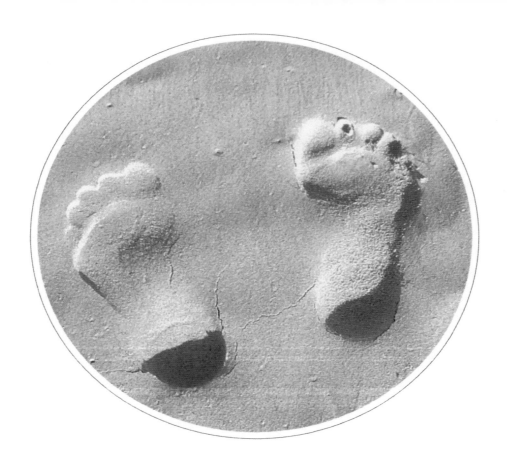

Existence

"Fact, state of living or having
objective reality"

Footprints in the sand,
reminds you of your intentions
you set for yourself
at the start of every year.
Stand firm and make a good impression.
When the tide washes over,
move on to create another footprint,
as the past is only a memory.
Ground yourself and feel the healing.

Harmony

"The harmonious blending of
colours and sounds"

Nature's own heart shape leaf,
takes you to look within,
and bring joy that will
touch others to live in harmony.
Take a deep breath,
and fill the lungs with
a fresh breath of air.
Celebrate life
with heartfelt harmony.

Communication

"Sharing or exchanging information"

Be bold as the rocks,
Be free as the wind,
Be wild as the flowers,
Listen to the sounds of the ocean.
How you hear,
How you see,
Is significant.
Listen to what others say.
Be kind in your voice when responding.
Friendly and positive words
make a big difference.
when we communicate together.

Hope

"A feeling of expectation or trust"

As found when looking at a rainbow,
the sun's light through water,
displaying a spectrum of colours,
the magical feeling of a promise.
That is our optimistic state of mind.
When hopes are dashed many look
to the cross of hope, love and faith,
positive aspects of sacrifice,
through life's earthly journey.
The desire for peace and serenity.
Take time to smell the roses of love,
and gratitude.

Optimism

"Confidence about the future"

Think about that window with a view,
bright, fresh and colourful.
It is what you see and associate with,
that inspires your future.
Life is about energy and its vibration.
warm and fun loving like the colour orange.
Look to the Aloe plant that stands
tall with confidence for it has
the creative ability to heal.
The future looks optimistic.

Stability

"The state or quality of being stable"

With this comes abundance and happiness.
It makes me think of the Bottlebrush tree.
In the right environment it will survive,
well rooted, standing tall and firm,
with its striking brush-like flowers.
It awakens our passion of warmth,
as the red flowers look radiant in the sun.
I instinctively think of my family,
my base, to provide stability.

Imagination

"The act or power of forming a mental
image, new ideas or concepts of objects
not present to the senses"

Let this succulent flower
dazzle your imagination.
Connect with your spiritual self,
be it pink, violet or purple in colour.
It tends to draw you in,
and when the sun goes down,
the petals cover you
in that imaginary place,
of enlightenment.

Happiness

"A state of well-being and contentment"

Wow! A word that describes joy, pleasure,
cheerfulness and just being happy.
When the sun shines, be happy!
When the rain falls, be happy!
When the flowers grow, be happy!
I associate happiness with
the colour yellow,
the ability to perceive and understand,
a wonderful boost to my self-esteem.
Rejoice in this energy of happiness.

Good Health

"The state of being free from
illness and injury"

If only this could be true throughout life,
A goal worth striving for year after year,
that feeling of satisfaction,
when in good health.
This pinkish rose scented geranium flower,
has a universal colour to remind us,
to love oneself and others.
The tiny flowers symbolic of
our many organs and body parts.
The essential oil of the rose geranium,
considered balancing for the mind and body.

Timeless

"Not affected by the passage of time"

What seems like an endless
mountainous landscape,
with typical low scrub bushes
scattered among the rocky outcrops.
A vegetation found in the
Karoo region of South Africa.
As the sun forms shadows
across the landscape,
you cannot help but admire the
breathtaking views of the river gorge.
The clear waters of the river
standing still in time,
reflecting a mirror image of its surroundings.
There is no beginning or end to its beauty.

Fulfillment

"A feeling of pleasure and satisfaction
because you are happy with life"

Through the haziness my wisdom blossoms,
my knowledge gained through experience,
and happiness rooted within
my centred being,
a great sense of feeling and achievement.

Inner Peace

"A state of being mentally and
spiritually at peace"

A sense of calmness as you walk
along the beach,
with the sun reflecting light on the water,
the clouds casting shadows on the sand,
a time of transformation.
The sound of the ocean relaxes
your state of mind,
bringing that feeling of inner peace.

Gratitude

I have survived to tell the tale,
with the light house as my guide,
knowledge, wisdom and guidance,
I have completed my first book.
Many thanks to my son, Paul
and my dearest friends worldwide
who have supported me throughout.
Now it is time for new adventures.
Putting sail to the wind,
a new horizon awaits.
As I bid you all farewell
until my next journey.

Magazine Publications of my poems, artwork and photographs

'**United Colours of Design**' Founder is Amy Barroso (A magazine for creatives who share a love of colour)
The Copper Book – 01-01-2021. My poem and photographs on page 142, '**Copper Journey**'
The Red Book – 01-04-2021. My painting, photograph and prose on page 173, '**Family Connections**'

Book Publications of my short story and published poems

'**Memoirs of the Imaginative Mind**' Edited by Sarah Marshall (New Fiction book of short stories - 2004)
My short story on page 15, '**A Jacaranda Blossom**'

'**Poetry Now Eastern England 2004**' Edited by Natalie Catterick (An Anthology of Poetry - 2004)
My poem on page 68, '**Jacaranda Blossoms**'

'**9/11 The Memory Lives On**' Edited by Steph Park-Pirie (Poetry Now - 2004)
My poem on page 121, '**9/11**'

'**Expressions from London & Home Counties 2005**' Edited by Steve Twelvetree (Poetry - 2005)
My poem on page 119, '**Remember me this Christmas**'

'**Valentine's Verse 2005**' Edited by Chiara Cervasio (Poetry- 2005)
My poem on page 65, '**Oh! Be My Valentine**'

'**Poppy Field 2005**' Edited by Steve Twelvetree (Inspired poems of remembrance and reflection on the adversity of war - 2005). My poem on page 287 '**Remembrance Day**'

'**The Meaning of Christmas**' Edited by Sarah Marshall (Poetry - 2005)
My poem on page 1, '**Christmas**'

'**Celebrations**' Edited by Heather Killingray & Sarah Marshall (15 years of the People's Poetry - 2005)
My poem, '**Jacaranda Blossoms**'

'**Daily Reflections 2006**' Edited by Heather Killingray (Anthology of Poetry, Book Dedication – 2005/2006)
My poem on page 366, '**Alone**'

'**The Lovebug**' Edited by Annabel Cook (Love Poems - 2006)
My poem on page 7, '**Roses**'

'**Animal Antics**' Edited by Michelle Afford & Laura Martin (An Anthology of Poetry Celebrating the Unique Bond Between People and Animals 2006)
My poem on page 321, '**Bobs**'

'**Southern Poets**' Edited by Lynsey Hawkins (A Collection of Contemporary Verse- 2007)
My poem on page 34, '**Water Lily**'

'**Daily Reflections 2007**' Edited by Angela Fairbrace & Michelle Afford (Poetry - 2007)
My poem on page 53, '**A Vision**'

As the sun reflects,
a distorted roundness
through the clouds,
we are reminded of
the crazy times we live in.
Patiently, we await
a new dawn.

Cowes, Isle of Wight

Printed in Great Britain
by Amazon

11757384R00058